# Morgan the Magnificent

## STORY AND PICTURES BY

## IAN WALLACE

*Margaret K. McElderry Books*
NEW YORK

Every morning at dawn, when it wasn't storming outside, Morgan stole out of bed and climbed up onto the barn roof. Then, as the rooster crowed, she walked straight and sure across the tin peak and stood on her hands.

On her one hundred and sixty-sixth walk she was
caught by her father. "We'll have no more of that stunt,"
he told her, as she scrambled down to the ground.
　　"But, Daddy," she protested.
　　"No buts, Morgan. Now be off with you."

Morgan set about her daily chores. Grumbling, she collected the eggs that had been laid during the night, and milked the cows until the pail was frothing full.

"Some swell life this is," she said.

When her work was done she unfolded a large poster from her pocket. It announced the arrival of Amazing Anastasia and the Condos Brothers' Circus. Morgan pored over the picture of the daring high-wire artist.

She laid the poster down on the floor and climbed a ladder that stretched up toward the barn roof. There she walked back and forth across the highest beam until she could do it with her eyes closed.

That evening Morgan cartwheeled across the summer fields of the farm. The brown earth warmed the palms of her hands. Stopping where the land dropped down into a valley, she saw circus tents far below.

Morgan raced along the road and entered the circus grounds. She wandered about, gawking at the sights, until, in a far corner, she came upon an exotic tent. Peeking through the entrance, she saw something glittering in the dark like fireflies dancing on summer lawns. She stepped inside.

On a seamstress's dummy hung an exquisite costume. Morgan recognized it at once.

"It's Anastasia's dress," she gasped, and tiptoed forward. "One little touch won't hurt," she told herself.

A few minutes later, her own clothes lay at her feet, and Anastasia's dress hung loosely from her shoulders. A pair of fine leather shoes fitted her feet perfectly. Morgan picked up a parasol and looked in the mirror. A beautiful high-wire artist looked back. She knew what she had to do.

Outside, the roar of the crowd grew louder. Morgan could hear the ringmaster calling, ''Hurry! Hurry! One and all! The show is about to begin!''

Morgan followed a troupe of elephants to the main circus tent and tiptoed through the performers' entrance. The smell of sawdust, sweat, and wild animals filled the air.

It was the elephants' turn to perform. As Morgan watched them lumber past her into the ring, she realized that this was her chance. She danced and pranced behind them and suddenly there she was, in the circus.

She tossed her head back in delight and looked up toward the tent roof that soared even higher than the roof of the barn. At that moment she spotted it—a single taut wire stretched from one end of the tent to the other.

Without hesitating, Morgan scrambled up a ladder that led to a platform high above the dirt floor. The air was hot up there and still.

As Morgan balanced Anastasia's parasol above her head, the acrobats far below spotted her and brought the elephants to a halt.

Morgan's first step onto the wire was quick and sure.

She glided along. Halfway across she knelt and bowed to the crowd. There was clapping and cheering. A smile spread across Morgan's face. But when she tried to stand again, she couldn't move. The wire suddenly felt thin through the soles of her shoes, not at all like the wide, firm beam of the barn at home.

The cheering stopped abruptly.

Morgan managed to stand at last, but the wire was shaking wildly. She tried to grasp it with the toes and sole of one foot, while she waved the other leg in the air for balance. Her parasol swung frantically up and down.

Not a sound could be heard in the Big Top.

A clear, calm voice spoke into the silence.

"Grip the wire with both your feet and keep your body straight. Then bring your parasol up over your head and hold your other arm out to the side."

Across the wire on the far platform stood Amazing Anastasia. A fine gold chain sparkled around her ankle.

Morgan did as Anastasia directed. The wire gradually stopped shaking. Soon she was gliding forward once again.

When Morgan reached the other side at last, Amazing Anastasia kissed both her cheeks and the top of her head. As they turned and bowed to the screaming crowd, Morgan spotted her father far below, standing at the edge of the ring. He blew her a kiss.

Later that week Morgan and her father went to say
good-bye to the circus until next year. Amazing Anastasia
handed Morgan a small brown package. Inside lay the
pair of fine leather shoes with a card that read, "To
Morgan the Magnificent." As the circus wagons rolled out
of town, Morgan stood on her hands and her father
applauded loudly.

For Morgan Haupt

First published in Canada 1987 by Douglas & McIntyre/Groundwood Books, Vancouver/Toronto. Copyright © 1987 by Ian Wallace. All rights reserved.
Margaret K. McElderry Books, Macmillan Publishing Company, New York
First United States edition 1988
Printed and bound in Hong Kong by Everbest Printing Co., Ltd.
10  9  8  7  6  5  4  3  2  1
ISBN 0-689-50441-1    LC 87-15482    CIP data is available.
The original pictures for *Morgan the Magnificent* are watercolor paintings.